naked ladies

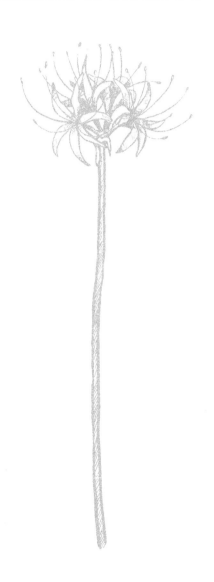

SOUTHERN MESSENGER POETS

Dave Smith, Series Editor

naked ladies

NEW AND SELECTED POEMS

Julie Kane

Louisiana State University Press

Baton Rouge

Published by Louisiana State University Press
lsupress.org

LSU Press Paperback Original

Designer: Barbara Neely Bourgoyne
Typeface: Proxima Sera

Cover illustration courtesy Adobe Stock/Cameron Ayn Carlson.

Poems herein have been selected from *Body and Soul* (Pirogue Publishing, 1987); *Rhythm & Booze* (University of Illinois Press, 2003); *Jazz Funeral* (Story Line Press, 2009; Red Hen Press, 2021); *Paper Bullets* (White Violet Press, 2014); and *Mothers of Ireland* (LSU Press, 2020).

Uncollected poems in this volume first appeared as follows, sometimes in a slightly different form or under a different title: *64 Parishes:* "Cane," "Mimosa," and "The Tree Keeps Weeping"; *Alabama Literary Review:* "Akhmatova"; *Barrow Street:* "Fusion at Sea" and "The Pale Green Moth"; *Christianity and Literature:* "The Old Irish Harpers"; *Connotation Press: An Online Artifact:* "Gift Horse: Ars Poetica"; *The Dark Horse:* "Colorific"; *Gris-Gris:* "Bass Voice," "The Dollhouse," and "The Lemon Juice Alphabet"; *JMWW:* "Elegy for a Performance Artist"; *Like One: Poems for Boston,* edited by Deborah Finkelstein: "In Summer My Father"; *Literary Matters:* "Across a Crowded Room"; *Maple Leaf Rag V,* edited by John Travis: "Jeep Pantoum"; *Measure:* "Ruby Red Opel GT"; *Mezzo Cammin:* "First Communion Album"; *Peacock Journal:* "Attenuation" and "Pink Magnolia"; *Per Contra:* "Lady's Slippers" and "Pecan Tree Stories"; and *The Recorder: The Journal of the American Irish Historical Society:* "Aftermath."

"The Old Irish Harpers" was set to music for SATB chorus, harp, and piano by composer Dale Trumbore as "The Sallow Harp." It was premiered by the Macalester College Chorale, directed by Michael McGaghie, on May 30, 2023.

Library of Congress Cataloging-in-Publication Data
Names: Kane, Julie, 1952– author.
Title: Naked ladies : new and selected poems / Julie Kane.
Description: Baton Rouge : Louisiana State University Press, 2025. |
    Series: Southern Messenger Poets
Identifiers: LCCN 2024033318 (print) | LCCN 2024033319 (ebook) | ISBN 978-0-8071-8374-8 (paperback) | ISBN 978-0-8071-8407-3 (pdf) | ISBN 978-0-8071-8406-6 (epub)
Subjects: LCGFT: Poetry.
Classification: LCC PS3611.A544 N35 2025 (print) | LCC PS3611.A544 (ebook) | DDC 811/.6—dc23/eng/20240816
LC record available at https://lccn.loc.gov/2024033318
LC ebook record available at https://lccn.loc.gov/2024033319

Contents

Jazz Funeral

Paper Bullets

Body and Soul

THE GOOD WOMEN

Three out of four
are named Mary,
these good Irish women
who surface at wakes
like earthworms after rain.
Death makes them bake
turkeys, casseroles,
applesauce cakes.
They breathe the thick
incense of flowers
for strength, dispense
prayers like milk
from each massive breast.
Black becomes them.
Red-haired, broad-hipped
for easy babies,
I stand among them,
betrayer of my race:
I whose God bless you's
have no authority behind them
am awkward as the corpse
in this army of grace.

VERONICA

What Veronica did with the cloth
the nuns never said.

Did she hang it over her bed
and stick palm fronds behind it annually?

Or did she
wring out the sweat and blood
on river stones, saying:

His is a sweet face, but how
can I dust, or dry the crockery

without my cloth?

WELSH PIETÀ

This Mary
has no composure.

Her nose is lumpy;
one suspects it runs,
despite the magnitude
of grief.

Not even her hands know
what pose to hold;

blame the sculptor,
unskilled in the basics,
the rippling of cloth;

no sure-fingered Michelangelo
would strip her of grace
and leave her

puzzled and dwarfed
in that vast choreography
of thunder and angels:

her dead boy
flopped on her knees
like some strange fish
she must clean and serve.

THIRTEEN

All summer she twirled
in pearls and satin gowns,
pale as a mushroom
in the attic.
Sometimes her aunt or
her father would hint that
the field of Queen Anne's lace
at the end of the road
was chock-full of children
her age. Her age
was suddenly uncertain as
the woman's breath
rising and falling
in an oxygen tent
all summer long.
Nothing to do but wait.
In the stale heat
of the attic, in the rippled
full-length mirror, she posed
in velvet, in chiffon,
in her mother's useless clothes:
waiting for her breasts
to blossom and fill
the loose bodice of her grief.

THE IRIS GARDEN

Flowers of time:
one the color of blood,
one pale blue and frilly
as an organdy gown,
one black as the soul
the nuns drew
in colored chalk.
If you dreamed an iris,
you would find it here.

You strangle
on the sweet air: it is
the room your mother left
for the party. Now
you leave for parties,
you leave
little ghosts of scent
behind you. Men
wear you like a rainbow
on their dark wool arms.

When your many colors fade,
bouquets of purple irises
will bloom beneath your skin.
You will lean to the earth alone.

ROSETTA

They wanted to
wallpaper the burn
with strips of thigh.
Leave it alone, you said:
this is the flower
I am bringing to the dead.

Men want you. You can't
get used to it. They can't
get used to the scar
no sequined G-string
can hide. They touch it
jealously: a pressed corsage
from your last lover.

You age around it.
Year by year, new veins
nudge and surface
for air. Rose and code,
text of petals, this rosetta
will teach you how to live
with your shame. When
men do not want you, when
rain comes to matter, it
will warn you of rain.

LASTLY, A WOMAN THINKS OF HER FACE

A woman whose face has failed her
flips her skirt like a two-headed rag doll.

Her new mouth is a Cupid's bow, a Barbie doll pout.
It is tongueless, and always calling, "Help!"

A woman whose new face fails her
turns on the gas in her dollhouse kitchenette
or takes too many pink candy pills.

Men blow their brains out.
A violent woman aims for the wrists,
for the thin stems fragile as tea party china.

Selfish as a pharaoh, a woman keeps her treasure
after death. Surely beauty matters!
It is bartered every day for emeralds and chocolates
and even an occasional kindness. Think of that!

Lastly, a woman thinks of her face. She dies
like a doll lying down to blink.

THE PANTRYMAN

Too old or too dumb
to come to work stoned
like the pastry boys and salad girls,
he came to work drunk
and got drunker,
on a six-pack in the cooler
by the Jersey tomatoes
and the California fruit.

But his knife stayed sober
while the lemon wheels
whirled in the air
above the cutting board,
obedient as worlds
spun into orbit, and
the dragons on his forearms
came to life again
with tricolored eagles
and serpents and fish.

If he was close enough to
stink, then you were close enough to
mind your own business
when you noticed
the scar above his elbow
where he'd gouged out
his ex-wife's tattooed name
like a bad spot
on a useable potato.

WAITRESS SHOE/HAIKU

1.

Each lady's slipper
full of pink champagne has a
twin, brimful of blood.

2.

Above its crushed-down
heel hangs a blistered heel, clone
of chin over bib.

3.

Other white shoes turn
gray; it turns the rose of the
roast juice dripped from plates.

4.

Breaking it in is
a myth like a hundred-buck
tip, though laces break.

5.

Cinderella's shoe
was fur, not glass, in French. Tried
glass? Come here. Try this.

DEAD ARMADILLO SONG

I've never seen a live
armadillo, but I drive

Route 90, where the shoulder's
littered with the colder,

deader little critters,
getting stiffer and stiffer.

They seem to have weights
like living room drapes

in their bottoms, for they lie
with their feet to the sky.

By God, there's a lot of 'em,
fat as stuffed ottomans,

World War I tanks snared
in terrorist warfare,

or small coats of armor
whose knights became farmers.

CRANBERRIES IN LOUISIANA

I stud my muffins
    with stones,

for that's what they are:
    little garnets

from my faraway home.
    How consoling it is

in this land of
    rotting figs

to encounter them:
    sour, red, jewel-y.

PRAYER TO CHAOS

Let the universe be random;

Let no choreographer impose
    design on the dance of atoms;

Let the stars' prophecies, the old dead light
    skew past our lives;

If the lines on the palms of our hands
    be life charts, let them swerve

like rivers when we touch;
    no, not touch: collide.

REASONS FOR LOVING THE HARMONICA

Because it isn't harmonious;

Because it gleams like the chrome
    on a '57 Chevy's front grille;

Because it fits in a hobo's bandanna;

Because it tolerates spit—
a little spit means the music is fervent;

Because it's easily rigged
to a contraption that frees the human
    hands;

Because it's cynical, yet sings;

Because it sings breathing in.

NARCISSUS

He was looking for his face
in a city
where women dyed their hair
blue, and men
limped by like cripples
on rainbow shoes
six inches high. More wine
was all I wanted,
but he dragged me into
every magazine shop
on the Champs-Elysées.

I was wearing
my silver sweater
and I glittered like
his perfect teeth.
He was lovely as an angel,
but the camera had his soul
and we couldn't find the ad
so he took me back to see
his portfolio.

On his street the red curtains
were drawn for the night,
the whores on their backs
pure as mirrors.
My God, but you're beautiful,
I told him, and he leaned
to kiss me in the city
full of pilgrims come to see
wonders of marble, miracles of gold,
monuments of no new angles.

VEGAS

The way the boxman tilts his head back,
pushing another fifty down the slot
in the table with an icy Lucite tool
as if he were grappling a body,

reminds me of a gambling man who grabbed
a scattered deck of cards and dealt out
five-card stud hands as a party broke up
without even thinking, a bachelor's habit.

I was starting to like him;
I asked him what was wild.
Dude in his alligator boots, he smiled
from the nose on down
and tilted back his head.
"I am, sweetheart," he said.

He drowned a week later.
The coffin was closed.
That's what they tell me, I didn't even go.
I came to Las Vegas where the rivers aren't real
to forget him, tilting back his head.

I will bet his final age
at roulette, 31,
before this night is over
34-to-1,
and it will hit
as if his elegant shadow
were spinning the wheel.

You tilting back your head.

Boxman, you devil, won't you meet my eyes?
You look like my lover who died a week ago.
The desert is a wreath of white chrysanthemums,
and you're the handsomest live man I know.

BLOND MEN

I think I ought to warn you
that I hate blond men
before you break your heart.

I hate the greenish gold
of their eyebrows and lashes,
how they shatter the sun
into rainbows.

And their eyes:
like a long drink of water.
That clear and that cold.

Worse than the eyes,
worse even than the old
gay men wanting the same
smooth cheeks and chests
and staring me down in public,
dueling with me for that innocence,

is the blond hair—
back to our subject—
the shock of a bright blond head
slanting above me like a sunbeam
on the covers of my dark blue bed.

THE ACCIDENT

I wonder whose bottom he patted
rising out of bed
at two o'clock in the morning
the night I wrecked

my car running into an oak tree
on Annunciation Street.
Maybe nobody's bottom, my ghost
still white-on-white on the sheet.

The ghost beside me was steering
when I hit that gnarled,
moss-hung oak. I don't
remember the turn on St. Charles

from Carrollton, or why
I picked him out to phone
six months after the breakup,
like another of his grown

children wrecking their lives.
Of course, when he came, he joked
at how good my aim was
with the neighbors in their robes,

called the cops and a tow truck.
Of course, he didn't ask
what had happened, seeing the car
and the tree and the path

between and the laws of physics,
which do not bend for oaks.
That's why they have to be smashed through,
sometimes, body and soul.

LOVE POEM FOR JAKE AND ITHACA

The bedroom window had a telescope
set up in front, but other than that,
the room was a typical student's room:
blacklight posters or Peter Max,
a bookcase made of cinderblocks.
There was only one book of poetry:
Comic Epitaphs from Country Graves.
I knew he wasn't the man for me,
though he always got up first to toss
our blue jeans on the space heater grille,
there being no heat in the upstairs rooms,
and sometimes he dressed me under the quilt.
I wanted to be a poetess,
pale, with a shock of copper hair,
drinking Jack Daniels on the rocks
and dying too young with love affairs
like Hollywood credits behind my name.
And so I crumpled paper up
and stubbed out Marlboros one by one
on the melting sides of a styrofoam cup.
He always wanted to show me things
through the telescope: a white-tailed deer
in the field out back, a blizzard sky
into which the barn had disappeared.
I tried not to let my annoyance show.
Sometimes he strapped his snowshoes on.
I remember his lonely figure tracking
down a hill toward the lake beyond
as I stood in the window tapping out
a line in my head with a cigarette.
I thought I had places to go alone.
If I could stand in that window again,

I would throw on my scarf and winter coat
and follow the trail his snowshoes make
over the fields of falling snow
and down to the glacial lake.

Rhythm & Booze

MARASCHINO CHERRIES

Three little girls on the morning after,
out in the kitchen poking around
for cherries soaked in whiskey like a bomb
of grown-up secrets. Other times we found,

by Mom's clip earrings and kicked-off shoes,
blue glass monkeys on swizzle sticks,
doll-sized Oriental parasols,
cocktail napkins with jokes we didn't get.

Cherries as precious as Burmese rubies:
Once in awhile, while the grown-ups slept,
we ate our fill of cherries from the jar,
but even then we liked the booze ones best.

KISSING THE BARTENDER

The summer we kissed across the bar,
I felt sixteen at thirty-six:
as if you were a movie star

I had a crush on from afar.
My chest was flat, my legs were sticks
the summer we kissed across the bar.

Balancing on the rail was hard.
Spilled beer made my elbows stick.
You could have been a movie star,

backlit, golden, lofting a jar
of juice or Bloody Mary mix
the summer we kissed across the bar.

Over the sink, the limes, as far
as you could lean, you leaned. I kissed
the movie screen, a movie star.

Drinks stayed empty. Ashtrays tarred.
The customers got mighty pissed
the summer we kissed across the bar.
Summer went by like a shooting star.

VILLANELLE FOR THEL

The night he took me up against the wall,
the veins on his neck standing out like ropes,
I learned that life is not like books at all.

I was nineteen when I started to ball
politely with poets and bookish folk,
but in my thirties up against the wall,

bashing and banging like a poor rag doll
with a candy heart and no brains or bones.
I saw that life is not like books at all,

but more like headlines—barroom brawls,
a blues song sung with flatted notes—
the night he took me up against the wall.

Uncomprehending, my mother calls
my poems "vulgar" on the telephone.
She taught me how to read when I was small.
I tell her life is not like books at all.

THE BARTENDER'S ARMS

Something unusual about his arms,
framed in a T-shirt with cutoff sleeves,
drew my attention behind the bar:

gold fuzz, babyfat, raised pink scars,
the rose tattoo in blue and green.
Something unusual about his arms.

Voices and asses and eyes had charmed
me previously, but arms? Good grief!
The way his shoulders drooped behind the bar,

as if he were a kitten in its mother's jaws,
front paws dangling, got to me.
Something unusual about his arms.

My own right mind and my upturned palm
warned me it would end in grief,
and still I leaned my elbows on the bar.

When I am eighty, wise, and calm,
and take this yellowed poem out to read
with liver-spotted hands and flabby arms,
I will be cured of men and bars.

BAR NOISE

A blast of bar noise on the telephone.
Is the ceiling tin? Is the mural Fess?
He doesn't know where he is. I'm home.

So much for spending the night alone:
nightgowned, pimple-creamed, getting some rest;
the seven digits of my telephone

deep in his brain as breathing on his own.
Blanket to couch, I make a nest
to wait for him till he gets home.

On a bar napkin, in a hand unknown,
somebody copies my street address
from the chained book by the pay phone

to give the cab. He's a boomerang thrown
on the night's savanna, returning to the breast
that launched him. That's the doorbell, not the phone,
and it's his body, but nobody's home.

THE BARTENDER QUITS DRINKING

The Mater Dolorosa parking lot
is always full on Fridays during Lent.
I hear them chanting Stations of the Cross

as I double park for the pastry shop,
this boozeless season giving us a bent
for doughnuts, candy, soda pop.

Twenty years ago, a schoolgirl, hot
in my coat, a lace mantilla on my head,
I swayed like them through Stations of the Cross,

thinking about forbidden choc-
olate ice cream, and dreading the dinner ahead:
fishsticks parceled out in meager lots.

Though I am not one of the good who got
a smudge of ashes to make amends
to Jesus for his time on the cross,

it's funny how the drinking stopped
to coincide with the start of Lent.
I mark each sober day with a cross.
I wake to joy in a season of loss.

THE MAPLE LEAF BAR

I wanted to understand the place:
the pressed tin ceiling and the out-of-tune
piano where the late James Booker played

in a rhinestone eyepatch and purple cape.
Bottles in sunlight like Arabian jewels:
I wanted to understand the place.

Maddox asleep like a cat onstage.
Kittens asleep in the storage room.
Red Sox, Celtics, and Bruins played

in bars that kept my uncles late.
They came home singing until they puked.
I wanted to understand the Saints.

What did you think, with your boyish face,
a bar rag tucked in your blue-jeans loop,
giving me all your change to play

the jukebox with? Another cra-
zy barfly making eyes at you?
I wanted to understand the place,
to play with words like Booker played.

ANGEL OF BARS AND NIGHTCLUBS

Angel of bars and nightclubs,
Stick to him like a shadow
Thrown by a fishnet candle
Or a neon sign in a window

Lead him past the fighters
Cover his battered nose
With the feathers of one wingtip
Stick to him like smoke

Angel of pubs and taverns
Lead him past the bottles
Doubled along the mirror
Amber, topaz, emerald

Stick to him like music
And if his legs should falter
Swirl him into the folds of your robe
Past the boastful talkers

Angel of jazz and juke joints
Steer him past the women
Whose eyes go to the ear stud,
To the bulge, who do not love him

Stick to him like perfume
Guide him out the door
Past the marijuana smokers
Leaners on parked cars

Cups and straws in the gutter
Frat boys trying to puke
Angel of fallen angels
Angel of drunks and fools

HALLOWEEN ON THE NILE

Off Luxor on a ship, I watched
the English waltz in stolen sheets
and tablecloths. You would have thought
a meeting of the Arab League
was taking place. No ice for drinks.
Date palms swayed along the shore.
My party favor, a camel doll,
leaked sawdust from its saddle sores.

Back at home it was afternoon.
My boyfriend would be getting up,
checking the mail for news of me,
pouring a shot in a coffee cup,
thinking about the costume ball
that evening, how his tennis shoes
would look with glitter on the toes.
Best go out for Elmer's glue.

The loneliness we get at night
by water, with a rising moon,
can't be drowned in alcohol.
"Ah, Matthew Arnold, let's be true!"
I told the Valley of the Dead.
The tall Egyptian steward laughed
and kept on asking me to dance,
liking my pretty Irish mask.

BOOKER AGAIN

Booker is dead, but I still go
sit on the Maple Leaf patio

among the palmettos and elephant ears
to listen to music and have a few beers

and check on the pink hibiscus tree
firing its blossoms like flares at sea

late in the year. Mention his name
and the bar help repeats the same

handful of stories—how he vomited on
the keys one night and Big John

had to clean it up with a bar rag;
how the dope arrived by White Fleet Cab;

how he stood up once with his pantseat shitty.
Beauty is truth, but truth is not pretty.

THE MERMAID STORY

1.

We've all heard half of the fairy tale:
A mermaid rescued a drowning prince,
swam him to shore, then pined away
because she missed the weight of him

and the heat of his breath against her neck;
nothing at all like the trickle of cool
saltwater flushed from delicate gills
when she kissed the mermen back in school.

But since there are witches underwater
as well as over, within a year
she'd bargained away her tail for legs—
and her tongue, too, as legs were dear.

She married the prince. His body hair
tickled like beach grass parched in sun.
An eel grew where his legs forked.
(She couldn't speak this to anyone.)

2.

Back in the anti-universe,
a woman writer with two tongues
rooted to the floor of her mouth
like anemones has just swum

so deep with her freak tail,
the sea spins and her brain goes black.
We'll see if the tongue she bargained for
can send a message back.

CHESS WITH MY MOTHER

Maybe we'll get the chessboard out
when she comes home and play again,
the tray stand wobbling over her sheeted
lap like mine when I was ten

and sick, too sick to lie on the couch
in the living room and watch TV.
I remember the concentration in
her face, bent over the printed sheet

of rules for hours. Across the room,
seahorses moved in a saltwater tank,
graceful in water, as if a pair of
knights had jumped their plastic stands.

In the beginning she always won:
I couldn't tell where the game left off.
Drifting in and out of my skin,
I heard her rattle the kitchen pots

or thought I heard her gliding like
a queen across the checkered floor,
up the dark diagonals
of linoleum tile, and out the door

where Dad was coming home, one stately
sidewalk square at a time, our king.
Time went by. I tried my shaky
legs again and started to win

and she lost interest. Set up the board:
Here's a penny for the missing rook.
Here's a button for the missing pawn.
Pawns are children trying to be good:

They start out running, then catch themselves.
They never go past the end of the street.
Like all small children, they want to be hugged,
but love is what drops the queen.

THE BOTTLE FACTORY

The summer after high school, seventeen,
I hired on at the bottle factory
in Nutley, New Jersey, to pack the lines
spun out by middle-aged Italian women
operating silkscreen machines. The work
was dumb: unfold a cardboard carton, place it
upright on a stand, insert a spacer,
pack a tier of tiny eyedrop bottles,
roof the bottles with a sheet of cardboard—
simple as layering lasagna noodles.
Each time a box was full, I'd heave it
off the stand, seal the flaps with masking tape,
start over—the only real excitement
coming from running too low on boxes,
wondering whether the boy would bring more
before my bottles toppled on the floor.

I liked to watch the women twirling up
blank bottles from the bin and wedging them
between two pins, which rolled the bottle surface
under the silkscreen. Telling dirty jokes,
scratching themselves under cotton muumuus,
humming along to the theme from *Tommy*
(which came on right before the hourly news,
because the deejay could interrupt it),
they worked so fast their fingers were a blur.
Every so often a machine broke down,
and packer and operator had to scrub
defective bottles with acetone rags
until the maintenance man could fix it.
Nodding off to sleep from the acetone,
my rubber gloves as holey as Swiss cheese,
I drifted in and out of bottle dreams.

The day I turned eighteen, the legal age
to operate equipment in New Jersey,
the foreman put me on my own machine:
a slower model, off in a corner,
the size of a Chevrolet stood on end.
And so I turned out Wella Balsam bottles—
hair conditioner, brown and orange—
and sent them down my own conveyor belt,
humming along to the theme from *Tommy*.
I wasn't fast enough to need a packer
and, anyway, it wasn't automatic,
powered by foot pedal, moving when I moved,
a bashful, lummoxy dancing partner.
I learned to twirl each bottle for inspection,
to scrub a flyspeck from a dirty screen
with cotton rags wrung out in gasoline.

I wanted to be as fast as they were:
to break eight thousand, at least, like the slowest
worker, Delores, who stamped gold leaf
onto April Showers talc. All day I raced
my best day's total, or her worst. Of course,
I wasn't Italian, or middle aged;
I didn't live just outside of Newark
(still smoldering from last summer's riots);
but I still longed to be good at something
physical: not words, but bottles.
I can't explain why it seemed important
or why, for years after that, I cruised
strange drugstores looking for bottles I'd made,
when love turned ugly, when words did not behave.

ODE TO THE BIG MUDDY

1.

Because I grew up a half-hour's drive
from the north Atlantic, always within reach
of the dried-blood-colored cranberry bogs,
the ice-bucket water, the desolate beach
with its circular rhythms, I looked down
on linear things, so like an erection
straining against a blue-jeans zipper,
always pushing in the same direction,
spine for brains. But I have learned to mimic,
quick for a girl, the river's predilection.

2.

The first time I saw the Mississippi,
under the curving wing of a jet plane,
it lay there listless as a garden slug:
glistening, oozing, brown. Surely Mark Twain's
paddlewheel visions, Hart Crane's hosannas
to the Gulf, Muddy Waters's delta blues
hadn't sprung forth from a drainage canal?
"Fasten your seatbelts for descent into
New Orleans. Looking to the left, you'll see
the Mississippi River"—so it was true.

3.

Unlike the ocean, the river's life is
right on the surface, bobbing there like turds:
a load of tourists on the *Delta Queen*
drunkenly singing half-remembered words
to show tunes played on steam calliope;

the push-boats nudging at oil tankers;
and nothing underneath but chicken necks
in crawfish nets, and our own dropped anchors.
The sea is our collective unconscious;
the river our blank slate, growing blanker.

4.

And yet the river gathers memories:
the ugliest things grow numinous
over time—the trail of a garden slug
crystalline, opaline, luminous
when the garden slug itself has gone
as the river itself will one day go,
already trying to change its course—
an afternoon we watched the ferryboat
go back and forth until the sun went down,
skimming the water like a skipping stone.

5.

Or the morning we gave back Everette's ashes:
homeless alcoholic poet-prince.
A cold March wind was ruffling the water.
Wouldn't you know, the ashes wouldn't sink;
so someone jumped in to wrestle them under.
It hit me then: I didn't want to die.
And so I made a choice, against my nature,
to throw my lot in with that moving line:
abstract, rational, conscious, sober—
cutting a path through human time.

VILLE PLATTE VILLANELLE

This is to inform you that I pissed
on the frozen soil of your hometown
Thanksgiving morning, and thank God I missed

my underpants and shoes and Silken Mist
L'Eggs panty hose, bunched up around
my ice-blue ankles as I pissed

on the landscape of your parents' tryst,
your first few steps—O hallowed ground,
now consecrated!—and thank God I missed

a pair of handcuffs on my wrists,
a turkey dinner in the Ville Platte pound
served up by deputies who might be pissed

I'd pissed and, therefore, by extension, dissed
the place that they were from, a one-foot-round
turf plug of it, now Agent Orange–crisped.

This is to inform you that you've kissed
a criminal. The restrooms were shut down
Thanksgiving morning in Ville Platte. I pissed
on dirt as frozen as your heart, but missed.

VILLANELLE FOR JOE, ON MY BIRTHDAY

For once you're going to be like other guys,
not call me even though you said you'd call
to wish me happy birthday. My "surprise"

will be a silent phone and bloodshot eyes,
a soggy Kleenex wadded in a ball
because you're going to be like other guys.

Beginning in July of eighty-five,
for all these years your reedy Southern drawl
has wished me happy birthday—no surprise,

a sort of Northern Star to plot course by
through middle age, its map of losses, all
that makes us, once unique, like other guys.

An old pop record—*Judy's Turn to Cry?*—
that you, my fellow Boomer, would recall,
expressed it: *What a birthday surprise!*

You'll stand me up and won't apologize
this year, old friend, but only by default.
You had to die to be like other guys,
your constant heart, time's loveliest surprise.

AFTER READING PO CHÜ-I

Like that old scholar-poet,
I've been posted to the far northwest to serve my state.
The only man in town who talks to me lives in his car
with a velvet tub chair and jars of peanut butter and jelly.
He says his ex-wife has money.
I have time to arrange my poetry books in alphabetical order.
In the mornings I sit out back longing to fluff the pink mating plumage
cascading down the neck of a little blue heron,
and in the evenings I sit out back watching car lights flickering in the river,
each fragile gold ingot a family coming home from the cinema.
When my friend comes from the capital to visit me in his BMW,
his high-performance tires quivering on the brick streets of my village,
we do not raise a cup of wine to the quarter moon
because this hard-won clarity has its own enchantment,

ANTS ON THE HUMMINGBIRD FEEDER

They won't cross a chalk line, he said, so—
Being a teacher and having a boxful on hand—
I stood on a lawnchair and daubed at the cottonwood's lowest branch
until there was a white ring around it.
But the branch was three-dimensional, not flat like a sidewalk,
and the ants cut a double-lane Ho Chi Minh trail
through knob mountains and peeling-bark lowlands
where the chalk line had missed.

Ants, said my bird book, *can be stymied*
in their attempts to take over a hummingbird feeder
by coating a section of the hanging wire
with petroleum jelly, mineral oil, or vegetable shortening—
So I stood on the lawn chair again
mounding fingerfuls of Vaseline
onto the inch-long S-hook—
and it worked for a couple of days, just until
there were so many bodies piled up in the Vaseline bog
that the living were able to cross on the backs of the dead
the way the French crossed the trenches of Verdun.

Make the wire longer, said a voice—
not that of the ants' angel—
so I unbent a coat hanger to its full length,
buttered it with Vaseline, and stood on the lawn chair again
hooking one end to the tree and the other to the feeder.
That did it! The ants surrendered
just as the rubythroats were starting to leave town
for the orchards of Costa Rica,
indifferent to the winner's cup
so many had lost their lives over.

NAKED LADIES

> Spider Lily: This hardy bulb has a curious habit of blooming on bare
> stems with no foliage present, which has earned it the common names
> "naked lady" and "surprise lily." It is also dubbed the "hurricane lily," as
> it tends to bloom during hurricane season in the U.S.
> —*Better Homes & Gardens* website, bhg.com

After the first rain
in October, they spring up
in straight rows around

houses and grave plots;
something in their DNA
craves a human-drawn

line to follow, like
grade-school children writing their
names on a ruled page.

Up close, too, they look
more like kids' toys than like *real*
flowers: red plastic

pinwheels fastened to
green wooden sticks, with not one
wan leaf among them;

and in their centers,
where you'd expect to find sex-
ual organs and

sticky gold pollen,
is only nothingness, like
the crotch of a doll.

Yet when I go to
the poor Creole church at Isle
Brevelle this time of

autumn for their fair,
it's not the store-bought aster
nor the rich man's rose

that I find tucked in
the plaster folds of Mary's
dress with a child's hope.

EGRETS

You have to love them
for the way they make takeoff
look improbable:

jogging a few steps,
then heaving themselves like sacks
of nickels into

the air. Make them wear
mikes and they'd be grunting like
McEnroe lobbing

a Wimbledon serve.
Then there's the matter of their
feet, which don't retract

like landing gear nor
tuck up neatly as drumsticks
on a dinner bird,

but instead hang down
like a deb's size tens from
the hem of her gown.

Once launched, they don't so
much actively fly as blow
like paper napkins,

so that, seeing white
flare in a roadside ditch, you
think, trash or egret?—

and chances are it's
not the great or snowy type,
nearly wiped out by

hat plume hunters in
the nineteenth century, but
a common cattle

egret, down from its
usual perch on a cow's
rump, where it stabs bugs.

Whoever named them
got it right, coming just one
r short of regret.

Jazz Funeral

WHISKER

Suddenly, this barb growing out of my chin,
as sharp as the quill on a porcupine:
the fault of a middle-aged shift in hormones,
that dot of the Other in the yin-yang sign.
It's springing up fast as a giant's beanstalk,
so rapidly I worry that my face,
cut open, might yield one mile-long hair
curled up like a spool of measuring tape.
Suppose I stopped cutting it back each morning,
relinquished my scissors, Sisyphe on strike:
would it twirl from my jaw like a catfish's whisker,
a kingbird's *vibrissa,* a bighorn sheep's spike,
a frayed piece of line from a fight-weary fish?
If I can't be a Bishop, could I be a witch?

BITCH

"Oh, get yourself a life," my mother snapped
because I'd said "poor thing" about the mother
dog that came around to nose the cat
food set outside for strays, its dangling udders
all the flesh that wasn't crimped to bone
like pie dough to a pan, its fur in patches:
ringworm, or the mange. Three times I'd phoned
the pound, but always she'd outfoxed the catchers,
weakened as she was. My mother, pooped
from shopping Jackson Square for peacock feather
masks, sipped sherry in my living room
and lost her houseguest manners altogether:
"Get yourself a life," is what she said,
but, listen: I'm alive and she's long dead.

PLAYER PIANO

"Common as dirt, the TVs of their time,"
the used piano man in Boston sniffs
at my grandmother's twenties player piano
as I itemize the house, executrix,
insulting the Kane family heirloom that
I thought would make us rich, its wood veneer
now black as the mold on Irish potatoes
that brought all our sorry forebears here
to work in factories or drive a team,
on holidays to sing and get besotted
around the piano my grandmother bought,
its flap valves and leather bellows rotted,
but still, amazingly, in tune—one key
gone soundless as, at the appraisal, me.

CARDINAL

This time last winter I abandoned you
or, rather, left you in the hands of God
and college kids demolishing my house
while I was teaching poetry abroad.
My last day home you came to feed at dusk,
your habit, bird of shadows, too exposed
in undiluted sunlight, malformed wing
draped rakishly as a dandy's cloak.
And though, back home again, I look for you,
I know deep down that was the final time.
What else was I to do? Not go? Take you?
To cage a songbird is a federal crime.
The yard is full of birds whose wings are whole,
but I can't recognize a single soul.

15 MARCH 2003

"Beware the Ides of March," a seer said
to Caesar, back when death was hand-to-hand.
This year, two hundred thousand U.S. troops
camped on Kuwaiti and Saudi sand,
each with a dog tag tucked in a boot
and a belt-packed, camouflage poncho/shroud;
and still you breathe the fluid in and out,
preparing to breathe air just months from now.
No blood relation—though you grow inside
my sister's womb, and she and I share genes—
as much the product of technology
as laser-guided bombs and M16s,
you pull us toward the future, unborn niece,
as small and fragile as the hope of peace.

DEATH OF A NEWSMAN

In Memoriam, Edwin Julian Kane (1924–2000)

The night sky is bright with the grieving Pleiades,
rising in the season your voice was stilled at last,
though sound itself never dies, your every newscast
spiraling out through space to distant galaxies.
When I was little, I thought you knelt in TVs.
I walked around them looking for a door and latch.
Heads jerked in swordfish-netted restaurants when you asked
for a menu. Women sent you cold remedies.
News of the ancient gods precedes your voice through space,
bulletins about rapists and transformations,
sisters scattered to stars, riding on waves of sound;
briefly, your news of protests, assassinations;
then, in the wake of your inimitable bass,
towers struck and destroyed, a much-loved city drowned.

FIRST RE-ENTRY, POST-KATRINA

As if a friend you used to see a lot
but haven't, lately, stops you on the street,
and right away you note the baseball cap,
the skeleton that has begun to peek
through facial features, and you hear about
the son or daughter in from out of town,
the chemo up at Willis twice a week,
how hard it is to keep a milkshake down:
The City Care Forgot (and then recalled)
comes into focus from your moving car,
whole blocks of houses with their doors kicked in
and rooflines covered with blue FEMA tarps,
and though the specialists must have their say
you see yourself it could go either way.

A HOBO'S CROWN FOR ROBERT BORSODI

(1939–2003)

Raised by his grandfather—the Depression-era philosopher Ralph Borsodi—Robert Borsodi graduated from Choate and the Yale University School of Drama, then turned his back on his privileged background. He opened a string of Beatnik-style coffeehouses throughout the American West, walking out on each one when the urge to wander struck him. He arrived in New Orleans in the 1970s and more or less stayed, although he shut down his coffeehouse to hop freight trains every summer and moved its uptown location three times before settling in a former crack house on Soniat Street. He continued to write, produce, direct, and act in plays for the benefit of his coffeehouse patrons; during the 1980s, he took his ragtag troupe to New York City several times and enjoyed brief runs off-off-Broadway. Terminally ill with bone cancer and lacking health insurance, he committed suicide by jumping from the Hale Boggs Bridge into the Mississippi River on October 25, 2003.

1.

Warm as a campfire on a bitter night:
that was your vision of a coffeehouse,
so, even though they were passé back then,
you set up shop and hung your shingle out
and gave bohemians a place to go
like Frisco in the fifties: bongo drums
and cool cat daddios and felt berets
tipped rakishly on brows of Dharma bums.
Who would have guessed that, twenty years ahead,
we'd find one popping up on every block,
a mocha latte filling every mug,
if not the chicken gracing every pot
once promised by a Dust Bowl populist
in times that fit you, that you somehow missed.

2.

In times that fit you, that you somehow missed,
your father's father, Ralph Borsodi, built
two model self-sufficient villages
among the Great Depression's Hoovervilles;
wrote treatises on canning, weaving clothes,
the upper-limit size of neighborhoods.
They say he raised you, when your parents split,
to shun big business and consumer goods,
which might explain why you would never shop
in stores (preferring curbside garbage cans),
or take a razor to your waist-long beard,
or stand in judgment of your fellow man,
although, at night, inside your coffee shop,
you heard the guns of urban rage go off.

3.

You heard the guns of urban rage go off,
but Nancy, in the shower, heard a CRACK!
and felt an object whack her in the head
while mourning you and worrying you'd laugh
to greet Anubis in the Hall of Truth,
a feather trembling in his weighing-cup,
and make him angry at your lack of faith
in anything but too, too solid stuff.
But back to Nancy, worried for your soul:
she found a piece of plastic by the drain,
no bigger than a Harrah's poker chip,
not broken off from fan or ceiling paint,
and guessed you meant to tell her she was right
about the jackal-god and afterlife.

4.

About the jackal-god and afterlife
you didn't worry, having lots of time,
unlike the patrons of the coffeehouse
who watched your beard grow as they stood in line—
the new ones, college kids or tourists armed
with guidebooks claiming that the place was cool,
who wondered how the words "Mu tea" could take
eight minutes to propel you off your stool
to pour hot water in an ancient cup.
Well, hell: they had the parrot overhead
for entertainment. Parrot-keepers know
that chances are they'll be the first one dead.
Your deathlike silence made my tongue go slack.
I'd blush bright crimson when you stared me back.

5.

I'd blush bright crimson when you stared me back:
no veiling secrets with a redhead's skin.
My surgeon said the melanoma wards
were full of victims who could be my twin,
"My people!" as the Ugly Duckling cried
on glimpsing snowy plumage through the reeds,
or Sherlock's carrot-crested villain thought
on seeing posters for the Redheaded League.
Your beard was reddish, but your tumor bone;
your cancer hidden, as my own was plain;
your odds were zero, mine were two in three;
so many of us gone, who signed our names
each New Year's Day inside your ledger-book
and ate your black-eyed peas to bring us luck.

6.

We ate your black-eyed peas to bring us luck,
your slimy cabbage, and the lumps of dough
you called "croissants," but which resembled, more,
the kind of biscuits kept on hand to throw
to man's best friend for shaking the right paw
or begging. Beggars can't be choosers, though:
the food was free, the poets out in force
from uptown mansions and downtown skid row.
And meanwhile, on a hundred other blocks
with windows made of glass, not plywood boards,
PJ's and Starbuck's and Rue de la Course
rang up sales of peppermint and eggnog
holiday coffees, muffins big as heads,
bombarding every sense to steal our bread.

7.

Bombarding every sense to steal our bread,
your rivals focused on the bottom line,
while you got by and even bought the house
your shop was in with coffee-can-chunked dime
and nickel tips. You never told
a soul your pedigree was Choate and Yale,
filled applications out left-handed so
they'd take your dungarees and ponytail
for working class and not New Haven chic.
From time to time you worked construction jobs
between the walked-away-from coffee shops—
eleven in as many cities, Bob,
all named "Borsodi's," in your one salute
to patriarchy and the men in suits.

8.

To patriarchy and the men in suits
I might have toasted when I met a tax
attorney in Borsodi's coffeehouse
who'd snuck in brandy in a silver flask
back then when anything could happen, when
the yarrow stalks were rolling hexagrams.
The tax attorney liked my poetry
or legs, and pulled a piece of marzipan
from one vest-pocket of his pinstriped suit
as, later, on his patchwork leather couch,
he'd tend to business like I wasn't there
and liquidate the surplus in accounts—
one scene of many from those crazy days
when we were players on Borsodi's stage.

9.

When we were players on Borsodi's stage,
our undisputed star was Sara Beth.
I saw her tap-dance in a hammock once,
jump in and out and never miss a step;
and once, in U.S. Army camouflage,
a plastic rifle in her doll-sized hands,
she sounded like a whole damn regiment
with Janet Jackson still in training pants.
I saw her, after you and she broke up,
performing for a crowd on Bourbon Street,
fat tourists throwing quarters as she tapped;
then Gary told me she had burned her feet
and needed money, and I wrote a check.
She wasn't in the write-up on your death.

10.

She wasn't in the write-up on your death,
but every summer you and she would lock
the coffeehouse and pack a few effects
to carry with you as you freight-train-hopped
to points out west where hoboes weren't extinct.
Who says you can't repeat a country's past?
You rode the rails to 1933,
where good faced evil over iron tracks.
Around the time the first Gulf War played out
on television like a game of Pong,
or maybe after Father Karl got shot
for pocket money as he walked his dog,
you gave it up for good, did not leave town,
lost track of who had won the hobo's crown.

11.

Lost track of who had won the hobo's crown,
that quaint Depression custom. You can bet,
these days, Reality TV would jump
to have the homeless court The Bachelorette
or seek apprenticeship to Donald Trump
by farting loudest after eating beans
or roasting rodents over Sterno cans
while chugging rotgut out of tin canteens.
They'd move the contest to a tropic isle
and slap up dummy trains and railroad tracks,
then bring in *Queer Eye*'s crew to renovate
bandanna pouches into Gucci sacks . . .
One thing we had in common, you and I:
pop culture was a train that passed us by.

12.

Pop culture was a train that passed us by
on tracks like those near the suspension bridge
from Destrehan to Luling, swamp to swamp,
on which they found your empty car, igni-
tion off; and Nancy said you might have hopped
a freight train, made it look as if you'd jumped;
you might be starting up a new Borsodi's
somewhere yet un-Disneyed and un-Trumped.
And when they couldn't find your body, I
kept hoping she was right, it wasn't real:
the divers dredging in the muddy river
under that stretch of rust-colored steel
that could have been designed by Frank Lloyd Wright
to look like part of nature on its site.

13.

To look like part of nature on its site—
a playwright's backdrop, while the divers searched
and Jimmy told us how you tried to see
a doctor when the pain kept getting worse,
but sat for days on end in Charity,
Art Deco palace for the dying poor,
while no one called your name, until you said
"the hell with it" and beat it out the door,
below carved figures that the government
bequeathed to us as anodyne for pain
when artists drew a paycheck from the state
and bullets hadn't ended Long's campaign,
then drove your flowered truck from friend to friend
to beg for help in bringing on the end.

14.

To beg for help in bringing on the end:
who wants to dwell on things like that when fate
lets up the pressure, lets us sit with friends
on common ground awhile and celebrate
what binds us to each other and a place
despite that whistle urging us to run,
despite the knowledge that a levee break
could level it like a one-megaton
atomic blast? You never lived to see
the halls of Charity entombed with mold,
dead bodies strewn like roadkill in the streets,
Borsodi's flooded like a toilet bowl.
Thank God for that, at least. We miss your light,
warm as a campfire on a bitter night.

PARTICLE PHYSICS

They say two photons fired through a slit
stay paired together to the end of time;
if one is polarized to change its spin,
the other does a U-turn on a dime,
although they fly apart at speeds of light
and never cross each other's paths again,
like us, a couple in the seventies,
divorced for almost thirty years since then.
Tonight a Red Sox batter homered twice
to beat the Yankees in their playoff match,
and, sure as I was born in Boston, when
that second ball deflected off the bat,
I knew your thoughts were flying back to me,
though your location was a mystery.

FINALE

How you'd begin was not always the same;
at times you'd even face me for awhile.
But always, in that drive before you came,
you'd flip me over, finish doggy-style.
Another funny thing: you'd never try
to steal a peek at me when I undressed.
I wondered if you'd rather have a guy,
if that was why you covered up my breasts.
Or maybe I was wrong, and you were straight,
but ex or mama used to yak, yak, yak;
you'd shove my mouth into the pillowcase
to face an uncommunicative back.
I haven't met her yet, your newest friend,
and yet I'd bet my butt about the end.

USED BOOK

What luck—an open bookstore up ahead
as rain lashed awnings over Royal Street,
and then to find the books were secondhand,
with one whole wall assigned to poetry;
and then, as if that wasn't luck enough,
to find, between Jarrell and Weldon Kees,
the blue-on-cream, familiar backbone of
my chapbook, out of print since '83—
its cover very slightly coffee-stained,
but aging (all in all) no worse than flesh
through all those cycles of the seasons since
its publication by a London press.
Then, out of luck, I read the name inside:
The man I thought would love me till I died.

Paper Bullets

MEN WHO LOVE REDHEADS

You can pick one out in a crowd
by the way he jerks his head
when an Irish setter passes,
drawn to that shade of red;
or the pickup line he utters
even to Raggedy Ann:
"If all your freckles merged,
do you know you'd have a tan?"

There are times you miss the clues
till you wake up after sex
to behold the nightstand photo
of his red-haired kids and ex;
then you know, for all of your charms,
he was only caught in the pull
of that least-known force of physics,
as a red flag draws a bull.

Some obsessives like girls plump
or missing a limb or two,
but the men hung up on redheads
are the men who prey on you.
Compared to men as a whole,
their numbers are very small,
yet without their kind in the world
you might never get laid at all.

ALAN DOLL RAP

When I was ten
I wanted a Ken
to marry Barbie
I was into patriarchy
for plastic dolls
eleven inches tall
cuz the sixties hadn't yet
happened at all
Those demonstrations
assassinations
conflagrations across the nation
still nothin' but a speck in the imagination
Yeah, Ken was the man
but my mama had the cash
and the boy doll she bought me
was ersatz
"Alan" was his name
from the discount store
He cost a dollar ninety-nine
Ken was two dollars more
Alan's hair was felt
stuck on with cheap glue
like the top of a pool table
scuffed up by cues
and it fell out in patches
when he was brand new
Ken's hair was plastic
molded in waves
coated with paint
no Ken bad-hair days
Well they wore the same size
they wore the same clothes

but Ken was a player
and Alan was a boze
Barbie looked around
at all the other Barbies
drivin' up in Dream Cars
at the Ken-and-Barbie party
and knew life had dealt her
a jack, not a king
knew if Alan bought her
an engagement ring
it wouldn't scratch glass
bet your ass
no class
made of cubic zirconia
or cubic Plexiglas
Kens would move Barbies
out of their townhouses
into their dream-houses
Pepto-Bismol pink
from the rugs to the sink
wrap her in mink
but Alan was a bum
Our doll was not dumb
She knew a fronter from a chum
Take off that tuxedo
Alan would torpedo
for the Barcalounger
Bye-bye libido
Hello VCR
No job, no car
Drinkin' up her home bar
Stinkin' up her boudoir with his cigar

Shrinkin' up the cash advance
on her MasterCard
and tryin' on her pink peignoir
Till she'd be sayin':
"Where's that giant hand
used to make him *stand,*
used to make him *walk?*"

EMILY, WALT, AND EDNA REWRITE "HEARTBREAK HOTEL"

Emily

'Tis down a Street—called Lonely—
That Guest House—where I dwell—
The Bell Hops' Tears—keep flowing—
The Guests—have Tales to tell—

Eons—since Baby left me—
To Desk Clerks—garbed in Black—
And I surmised—the Lodgers' Eyes
Weren't ever looking back.

Walt

I saw at the end of Lonely Street, with tear-filled orbs I mark'd it,
Saw the mournful hotel call'd Heartbreak, the lodge of the forsaken,
And I knew that, though it contain'd multitudes, I could always find a
    room there,
And I knew that it was a dwelling-place for broken-hearted lovers,
The bellhops weeping and moaning, and I longing to comfort them,
The desk clerks keening in black, and I longing to ease their sorrows,
To part the jet cloth from their bosom-bones and thrust my rude
    tongue athwart them.

Edna

I shan't be checking into that hotel,
Although some say there is a vacancy:
The somber occupants have tales to tell
And fain would blame their broken hearts on me.
Awake I've lain in every numbered room
Beside a husband of a single night
Who can do naught but weep away his gloom
Midst clerks in garments coloured anthracite.

Ask not why death forsakes this mournful inn
Whose lodgers grieve for my ephemeral charms,
Nor why I jilted them to lie in sin
Each weeknight in a diff'rent pair of arms:
Believe that ardour drew me to each man,
But Baby's got a short attention span.

THE LOST FASCICLE

128

Bring me the sunset in a cup—
And a Tequila Sunrise, while you're up.

204

A slash of Blue—
A sweep of Gray—
Paul Newman still
Grabs me that way.

213

Did the Harebell lose her girdle
To the lover Bee?
That is one Soft-Porn Flick
I don't care to see.

241

I like a look of Agony,
Because I know it's true—
If you're a masochistic Gent,
I'd like to paddle you.

317

Just so—Jesus—raps—
He—doesn't weary—
Eminem and Jay-Z
Are understandably leery.

333

The Grass so little has to do—
If you're watching it, that makes two.

341

After great pain, a formal feeling comes—
The Nerves sit ceremonious, like Tombs—
If your physician gives you Percoset
An altogether different high from Shrooms.

465

I heard a Fly buzz—when I died—
The swatter had been left outside.

485

To make One's Toilette—after Death
Has made the Toilette cool—
It's best to warm the Toilet up
When used as swimming pool.

525

I think the Hemlock likes to stand
Upon a Marge of snow—
They don't like to be stood upon,
The Marges that I know.

712

Because I could not stop for Death—
He kindly stopped for me—
The Harley should have tipped me off,
And the Hells Angels tee.

754

My Life had stood—a Loaded Gun—
In Corners—till a Day—
I had the Sense to empty it
And put the Shells away.

818

I could not drink it, Sweet,
Till you had tasted first—
You might be out to poison me.
I always fear the worst.

878

The Sun is gay or stark—
Gay as hell when it's dark!

1450

The Road was lit with Moon and Star—
And High Beams from some Asshole's Car.

1555

I groped for him before I knew
That he had but one Ball, not two.

1590

Not at Home to Callers
Says the Naked Tree—
Gentlemen, come calling!
Says the Naked Me.

THE RIVALS

There were only three contenders
For the great big poetry prize—
Two of the feminine gender,
My frenemy and I.
So we went to lunch, extenders
Of the peace pipe, civilized.

"You are so much more deserving,"
She said, "than little old me."
"I'm not fit to be your servant,"
I said, "at poetry."
Yet we both remained observant
For toxins slipped in our tea.

"If not this year, then later,"
My frenemy said then.
I said, "Once nominated,
It's only a matter of when."
But a lot can happen, waiting.
And how long—two years? Ten?

"But you know—I'm ten years older,"
She let slip over dessert.
"I've had *melanoma*!" I told her.
"*My* death is sure to come first!"
Then the room grew suddenly colder
And the versifiers, terse.

UNPLANNED OBSOLESCENCE

I wish I hadn't mentioned pay phone dimes
or female hurricanes, or pink foam rollers.
My poems slowly slip behind the times.
I wish I hadn't mentioned pay phone dimes.
Soon, editors will footnote all my lines
as coffin thieves pry silver from my molars.
I wish I hadn't mentioned pay phone dimes
or female hurricanes, or pink foam rollers.

PLEA BARGAIN

Inside the scanner's tunnel,
you swear that you will be
a candidate for sainthood
if spared from the big C.

You'll help to feed the hungry,
you'll comfort the bereft;
you'll minister to lepers
if there are any left.

But when the doctors tell you
that you are in the pink,
the terms that you agreed to
seem rather harsh, you think:

perhaps another kitten,
a shelter rescue pet,
or pound of fair-trade coffee
would settle up the debt.

Mothers of Ireland

INHERITANCE

They say that trauma's coded in the genes,
passed down to generations yet unborn
as thymine bases bond to adenines

and guanines throw a rope to cytosines
and brand-new double helixes are formed
with ancient trauma coded in the genes.

To watch one's children, with their mouths stained green
from eating grass till all the grass is shorn,
die one by one: do thymines, adenines

absorb the echoes of a parent's screams?
Too late, the boats of stony Indian corn.
Small wonder trauma's coded in the genes.

Like spools of film with horror movie scenes
in which our own progenitors performed,
those spiral loops of thymines, adenines

roll on inside us, soundless and unseen.
There's no escape, except not being born,
from trauma not our own but in our genes:
The Hunger, coffin ships, 1916.

THAT ONE OVER

Mary McCarthy Lynch (1867–1949)

She wore the china cabinet key around her neck
As if she couldn't trust even her long-time mate
To keep from making off with a gold-rimmed plate
To hock for whiskey money when he'd spent his check.
And what was inside the cabinet, to warrant theft?
China with chipped edges, "silver" that was silver plate,
A cut crystal jam jar she grandly called a "vase,"
A statue of Mary that a Lourdes priest had blessed.
Everyone else in town thought her man hung the moon:
She wouldn't even call him by his Christian name.
"That one over," she'd say, pointing across the room.
She made him sleep on the porch when he'd had a few.
To be Irish then was to be awash in shame.
He hadn't deceived her yet, but you never knew.

SECOND TIME AROUND

Back when I used to smoke, I'd stub them out
in crystal ashtrays all around the house

that turned my stomach, emptied in the trash.
Times when I slipped the last one from the pack

too late at night to risk a run for more
at some gas station slash convenience store,

I'd comb through ashes for the longest butts
and light them up again without disgust.

⌐

Minnie McCarthy scandalized the town
of Knockmullane, Cork, turning Jack Lynch down.

Pretty girls wanted American fun,
not boredom in Ireland with a farmer's son!

He followed her over and found her on her knees
scrubbing Protestant toilets for a couple bucks a week

and proposed to her again with no resistance met.
He was the longest butt she was going to get.

HER HEART

Julia Margaret Lynch Curtin (1896–1939)

My grandmother's sister Julia was born with a flaw in her heart.

The doctor's words to her parents tore like a claw to the heart.

Head of her bed by a window, no winter thaw for the heart.

Never to wed because childbirth would be the last straw for her heart.

Rumors her father punched at least one suitor's jaw for her heart.

But a redheaded traveling salesman would not withdraw from her heart.

Swearing his love was chaste and he'd keep hands off for her heart.

Swearing on Mary and Jesus with one freckled paw on his heart.

How could her bantamweight father not go soft in the heart?

Beautiful bride: such a chorus of ooh's and ah's from all hearts.

When her belly poked out it proved there is no law to the heart.

Julia's motherless boys would grow up raw in the heart.

THE JOHNS

Julia Agnes Glynn Kane (1890–1970)

It's true that my Grandma Agnes named three children John.

Living children, not dead: all bearing the name of John.

You might assume she was crazy about her husband, John.

But the truth is, following childbirth, she truly hated John.

Torn and bleeding, worn out, she'd put the blame on John.

When the nurse came around with the form, there'd be no sign of John.

Agnes would hiss at the nurse, "Oh, Christ! Just put down *John*."

Once she got home with the child, she'd grow attached to "John."

Then she'd begin to call him some name other than John.

But it caused some mix-ups at school that they were all named John.

And the draft board wasn't amused that they were all named John.

My Uncle Jim was the only son who was not named John.

He was named for Agnes's father, who was a James, not John.

James Glynn died on a mental ward surrounded by John Does.

Jim Kane was always a good boy, unlike the three bad Johns.

SAINT JOSEPH'S #2, NEW ORLEANS

Gregory Browne (d. 6 Sep. 1878) and Kate Manning Browne
(d. 5 Sep. 1878)

Dealers are trilling their lookout alarms
As I enter the city of the dead:
Row after row of gleaming marble tombs
In the middle of a bad neighborhood.

I am looking for Kate and Gregory Browne
Who died a day apart of yellow fever
Vomiting blood as black as coffee grounds
On Bourbon Street in the French Quarter.

Gregory was thirty, Kate twenty-five.
They would have been married two years at Christmas.
No record if they left behind a child,
My flesh-and-blood raised by charity sisters.

What drew them to this fever-ridden port,
Far away from any relative,
Doubly displaced from Galway and the North?
I had the excuse of marrying a native.

Foolish of me to think I'll find their names
Among grand temples to the Creole French.
Immigrant victims were dumped in mass graves,
Covered with lime in shallow dirt trenches.

Better get out of here before I'm robbed
Or find my Prius with the windshield smashed:
Not even rented space in oven-vaults
For poor Irish victims of Yellow Jack.

A pity no one searched their rented room,
Found an address, let distant family know.
All those years believing I was far from home,
So close to my great-granduncle's bones.

MY DOUBLE COUSIN ANNA

Anna Maria Hurley O'Mahony (1881–1972)

My double cousin Anna O'Mahony was a spy for her country.
She was Anna Hurley then, nearly forty, but not yet a bride for her country.

She would scout the British troops getting on and off trains at the Bandon
   depot.
Her farmhouse in Laragh stashed ammo and dispatches inside for her
   country.

One time she got raided and stuffed two IRA men under her dying father's
   bed.
"My father is dying in there: I pray you search quietly," she not-quite-lied
   for her country.

Anna's father Daniel, a Land League man, named her "Anna" for Charles
   Parnell's sister.
Anna Parnell, unlike her brother, never compromised for her country.

Anna Hurley's brother was a captain in the Third West Cork Brigade.
Shot in the back by Black and Tans, Frank Hurley died for his country.

Was it Anna who planted the plain iron cross by the Bandon River foot-
   bridge?
Silent reminder of a good man crucified for his country.

John O'Mahony went on hunger strike in London's Wormwood Scrubs
   Prison.
A big man, starved for sixteen days, he managed to survive for his country.

After the war was over, her father and brother dead, Anna married
   O'Mahony.
He was her link to the time she'd been most alive for her country.

To think she was still alive, past ninety, when I backpacked through
    Ireland at twenty,
Believing that no one over thirty knew a thing about the fight for a
    country.

FAMILY DRAMAS, ACT FOUR: THE CAVAN-TYRONES

I read that play in high school. Mrs. T.
Took morphine, but I knew the family well:
The language of their fights like poetry,

The silences like wind through stunted trees,
The drunken charmers and the ne'er-do-wells
Who couldn't charm the bitter Mrs. T.

The backdrop of a gray Atlantic sea,
As cold in August as a heart withheld,
Its rhythms those of Irish poetry—

O'Neill's own family drama spoke to me,
"The ponies" running like a carousel
Whose painted glitter holds out mystery

But finish line becomes infinity,
How habits shape of lives a villanelle,
The repetitions turned to poetry.

I pray to the quatrain to set me free;
We Irish know that language is a spell.
I read that play in high school, Mrs. T.
My fate without the grace of poetry.

MOTHER/MONARCH

Nanette Spillane Kane (1926–1995)

You with your brown pantsuits and flat shoes, so sensible;
Who would have guessed you'd come back as a butterfly?
But something in your house was always burnt orange:
A sofa, the basement walls, one zigzag in the collage
Of genuine South American butterfly wings
Whose artist must have been a heartless little shit.

None of your second-graders would dare say "shit"
In your classrooms—not if they were the least bit sensible.
But even the worst boys got a kick out of seeing wings
Emerge from jade-earring cocoons of monarch butterflies
Gathered each fall along roadside ditches collaged
With leaves colored red, yellow, brown, and orange.

My favorite high school minidress was striped black and orange.
I thought I looked "groovy," but I must have looked like shit.
I believed that a high hemline or low décolletage
Could save me from your fate of being drab and sensible.
The year I turned sixteen, I hatched into a butterfly.
In the back seats of Beetles, boyfriends pinned my new wings.

Between your force and my face, only a guardian angel's wings,
When rage at my rebelliousness made you see orange.
Your pretty young Irish mother had been a flirt, a social butterfly;
The grumpy old man she married, a bit of a shit.
You sided with him in the war of beauty versus the sensible.
Those were your mother's silks and powders, glued in your collage.

We propped it on the nursing home windowsill, that collage,
During the last weeks of your dying, when black and orange wings
Kept crashing into my windshield. I'd tell myself to be sensible;

Then I'd walk out into a parking lot and see a flash of orange
Lying in the gravel, bird-pecked, decaying like shit.
Soon your soul would fly out of your mouth, an Egyptian butterfly.

The winter after you died, twenty million monarch butterflies
Perished in a freak Mexican snowfall, their corpses collaged
On tree trunks in volcanic mountains, their beauty turned to shit.
How many canvases would you have papered with those wings?
Were you striking my face from beyond, by killing all that orange?
I write it down as if language could make it sensible.

FOXBORO SESTINA

My mother just wanted to get out of Foxboro
Where it was embarrassing to be Irish Catholic.
The priest kept his golf clubs in her parents' shed,
A blanket excuse to drop in for a drink.
Everyone knew everyone else's secrets
In that town of ten thousand with its central green.

Mayflower descendants once grazed sheep on that green
Smack in the middle of downtown Foxboro,
And it was a very badly kept secret
They'd burned down the first church built by Catholics
(So rinky-dink, its Crucifixion was only a painting).
Firemen just let it burn, as if it were some backyard shed.

Fires could have been quenched with the tears my mother shed.
Once, sent home from grade school with her stomach green,
She found her pretty young Irish mother drunk
In the lap of the duffer priest of Foxboro.
Seven years old, she began to hate being Catholic,
Though she kept what she saw that afternoon a secret.

How often she wished she could keep it a secret
That her Granny kept chickens in a coop behind the shed!
Protestants bought their chickens already plucked, unlike Catholics.
These days, it is cool to raise chickens and eat green,
But it was not cool when my mother lived in Foxboro.
She prayed they'd all drown in the trough where they drank.

My mother's Uncle Tim was the town's official drunk.
The brains of the family, Tim was rumored to have secretly
Taken the dental boards for his brother, in practice in Foxboro.
But once Tim started drinking, all inhibitions were shed.
He would serenade her friends from his spot on the town green:
Sad songs like "Kathleen Mavourneen," so embarrassingly Irish Catholic.

My mother escaped the town (though she raised us vaguely Catholic)
By marrying a dashing Irishman a bit too fond of drink.
For her 50th high school reunion, she returned to stand on its green,
Surprising us all with sentiment she'd managed to keep secret.
Did she sense the encroaching cancer, that looming watershed?
That last year, she drank from a mug that said "Foxboro."

I DREAMED OF BEING MOTHERED BY A CAT

I dreamed of being mothered by a cat,
Sunk in her plush as in a featherbed.
I'd never known a happiness like that.

My human mother's claws would not retract.
Even her language could unzipper red.
I dreamed of being mothered by a cat

Who'd give her life to save me from attack.
I sensed that fierceness in her as I fed.
I'd never known a happiness like that.

If there were siblings, I ignored that fact.
I had her to myself (or I forget)
The whole time I was mothered by a cat.

One dream can strike you like a thunderclap.
That mother cat, more goddess than a pet.
I'd never known a happiness like that.

The world was pure sensation, not abstract:
Some realm between the living and the dead.
I dreamed of being mothered by a cat
And something healed inside me after that.

WHORE

What kind of mother calls her daughter "whore"
when she finds out her daughter's fiancé
is moving in a couple months before

the wedding? Small-town priggish to her core,
smug priest who slams shut the confessional grate:
that kind of mother calls her daughter "whore."

Yet, when that husband battered down a door,
came crashing through a bookshelf barricade,
the daughter phoned her mother just before

instead of the police, or friends. What for?
The mother snapped, "Oh, don't exaggerate."
The phone line crackled with the unsaid "whore."

The daughter crumbled after the divorce.
She slept around as if each drunken lay
could blot out all the ugliness before:

so many men that she could not keep score.
They cradled her, if only till they came.
Once you have heard your mother call you "whore,"
you might as well be, if you weren't before.

YOU WERE SO GOOD

You were so good, you didn't make me sick
That first trimester that I carried you.
Not knowing there were two of us to feed,
I fed my change into the snack machine
Late afternoons at work, a change of habit.
Nights, TV couples joked about dead rabbits.

You were so good, you even let me bleed
That first trimester that I carried you.
The low-dose estrogen had made me spot
All month, so when I finally went off
And kept on spotting, never really flowing,
That's how I went so long without knowing.

You were so good, you must have been a girl
That one trimester that I carried you:
Trusting innately if you made no fuss,
Just kept your head down and were *good* enough,
I wouldn't let them cut you out like cancer.
I didn't ask your sex. I knew the answer.

PETIT MAL

"We could get married," I said, but I made him sick:
Not anything anyone else would notice,
Just a spell of petit mal that lasted seconds
But left him temporarily at a loss for words.

Not anything anyone else would notice,
But triggered more frequently at times of stress.
When he dumped me, it left me at a loss for words.
My life then was one big ball of chaos:

My workplace mired in scandal, my ex triggering stress
Late nights when he battered his weight against the door.
My life then was one big ball of chaos,
But a good man had loved me for almost three months.

I slept at his place to escape the assaults on my door.
Breakfast was home-baked bread with apple butter.
A good man, he loved me for almost three months.
When his bathroom was a darkroom, I had to hold my pee.

Coffee in bed, and bread with apple butter.
I was so happy with him, I knew it couldn't last.
He wore old lady underpants and sat on the john to pee.
His pickup truck was orange, his sneakers full of kittens.

I was so happy with him, I knew it couldn't last.
It had been over since March when I had to tell him,
Sobbing in the cab of his burnt-orange truck,
That I was three months pregnant and he was the father.

It had been over since March when I had to tell him
(Triggering a petit mal seizure that lasted seconds)
That I was three months pregnant and he was the father.
"We could get married," I said, but I made him sick.

TUNNEL OF LIGHT

Those who return report that, at the end
Of the tunnel of light, there's a receiving line
Made up of dead loved ones: relatives, not friends,
Blocking the gate to whatever lies behind.
It could be from a lack of oxygen,
A shared illusion as the brain cells die,
But it will still feel like it's genuine,
No matter if it's real or one last lie.
My mother waits there in her spider web:
No way around except by going through.
My little lost infant waits in her crib.
I don't fear dying, but I fear those two.
O holy mother, help us to forgive
Those who killed us and those who let us live.

DULLAHAN (BLACKOUTS)

With pity for all living things
Being chased by a ghoul on a horse
With its head tucked under its arm
Consider the plight of the rider

Consigned to blank nights on a horse
Or behind the wheel of an automobile
Consider the plight of the rider
Cruising the potholed streets of your city

Headless inside her automobile
Sheer muscle memory steering her home
Cruising the potholed streets of your city
Dullahan, headless Irish fairy

Drone-like, mindless, riding home
You may have sensed her, late one night
Dullahan, headless Irish fairy
Caught up in repetition

You may have sensed her, many nights
With your shamed red face in your hands
Caught up in repetition
With pity for all living things

GIVING AWAY THE LIQUOR BOTTLES

Home from college one Christmas, I packed
My dolls away in cardboard boxes,
Shutting their eyelids and smoothing their skirts
For the long sleep through time

Under the eaves of my parents' house.
How easily attachments go!
A moth flies out of the corpse's mouth.
In the end, we are dolls ourselves.

It was the same with my wedding dress
The day I gave it to Goodwill.
Do pharaohs wake in their tombs to find
Their jewels mean nothing to them?

Each step prepares us for the next.
Each loss prepares us for the last.
The hardest dolls to lose were glass,
That carton of outworn friends.

AA STORY

Across a hundred rooms with kiddie chairs,
Throughout a hundred mumbled AA prayers,
I wondered if your hugs were chaste as theirs.
Or tighter, closer?

You told your story once: old wealth, Tulane,
Those clubby breakfasts at the Pontchartrain,
Then begging on the beach for pocket change
In Pensacola.

Some nights we wound up partners, playing cards
In coffee shops we hung out in like bars.
You never knew if diamonds outranked hearts
Or hearts beat diamonds.

And once, because my car was in the shop,
You said you'd pick me up and drop me off.
You leaned so close to me, your breath felt hot
On my bare shoulder.

Who would have guessed we two would fall in love,
Or last until Katrina screwed it up?
Eleven years, three parents gone to dust,
And us still sober.

And now the time apart begins again,
Like film run backward, or a repetend
From fixed poetic form, and in our end
Is our beginning.

MY GREAT-AUNT GRACE

Grace Ellen Glynn Wild (1894–1941)

I would be lying where she lies if not for the grace of God.
That is the price for trying to drink a whole case of God.

She fell down a flight of stairs and fractured her skull.
"Complications of alcoholism," wrote the coroner in the space of God.

What shame did she bring her sisters, who would not claim the corpse?
She lay in the morgue six months. Slow is the pace of God.

When I was fat with cash, I tried to buy her a stone—
Forbidden in potter's field, which is not a place of God.

I stare at the wedding photo, my great-aunt's little fox-face
Radiant as if she had just glimpsed the face of God.

She married a sailor, was saved from a waitressing job—
But soon it was clear he was not from a race of gods.

"Straighten up or you'll end up on Dover Street"—
So warned the nuns of Boston, who were the chaste of God.

Her last address was a cold-water rooming house on Dover Street.
Carried out on a stretcher drunk, to the disgrace of God.

I carry her disease as I carry her middle name.
Written on paper, not stone, it cannot be effaced by God.

AS IF

As if the corpse behind the crime scene tape
Got up and took a bow where it dropped dead;
As if I got a phone call from the grave
And asked its occupant to share my bed.
Nine years ago, we fought and split apart
With our beloved city under water.
I turned to short-term lovers in the dark;
You moved in with a Southern judge's daughter.
I have to pinch myself to prove you're back,
Though balder, ten pounds thinner, better dressed—
As if the universe had jumped a track,
No hurricane, no choices second-guessed.
At times my ears pick up the strangest sound,
As if the dead were clapping underground.

THE SCREAM

I used to have a scream stuck in my throat
No matter what I did to jam it down:
Unswallowed pill on which I used to choke

No matter how much alcohol or smoke
I flung at it to try to wash it down.
I used to have a scream stuck in my throat:

Teakettle steam about to sing its note
Or seam of lava barely pressured down.
In desperation, I would sometimes choke

On random cocks to give the thing a poke.
Like tamping pipe tobacco farther down—
But still I had a scream stuck in my throat.

Not like a scream in nightmares, where no mote
Of sound escapes though monsters hunt you down:
In dreams, you want to make a noise, not choke.

This monster was still there when I awoke;
No earthly weaponry could bring it down,
Those years I had a scream stuck in my throat
Until I spoke my truth and did not choke.

New and Uncollected Poems

GIFT HORSE: ARS POETICA

There was nothing in my hand
    back then;

no carrot stub, no sugar lump
    to tempt you;

but you came to me at dusk.
    Out of the shadows

of birch trees, of crabapples
    you chose me,

and our first rides together
    were wild ones:

me with my fists knotted
    in your silk,

my knees clamped
    to your flanks;

desperate to last you out,
    to not get thrown.

Then I began to relax;
    my spine uncurled;

I could track what flashed
    in the branches;

and I sought out lessons
    from the masters

ahead of me, behind me
    in those woods.

You were always so finicky,
    would never once approach me

when the wind was rank with poisons
    from my skin,

and where I thought
    we were going

was seldom where
    you would take me

in those years before you let me
    bit and bridle you.

Half a century now
    bound together,

our rides slowed down
    to a measured canter,

the barn rarely out of sight
    as we round our turns,

how can I help but dread
    that white gate

looming ahead
    which I must

    leap across

unknowing: with you
    or without you?

FIRST COMMUNION ALBUM

In a white dress &
veil, white shoes & ankle socks,
hair copper as a

'52 penny,
she stares back from the concrete
stoop of a blue house,

unsmiling at the
grown-up behind the camera.
Shot after shot, in

the top right of each
frame, what looks like a ball of
flames floats above her.

"You & the Holy
Ghost," her mother used to joke,
riffling through pictures.

No joke to the nuns
in catechism class who
taught how it came down

to Christ's apostles
in licks of flame, bearing gifts
of tongues & vision.

A bad batch of film?
Her drunk father opening
the latched case outside?

Inexplicable
as the words that seem to come
not from, but through her.

LADY'S SLIPPERS

She had warned us not to
    pick them in the woods

or the police would come;
    so when we noticed

a new clump of them
    in her rock garden,

the delicate pink pouches
    speckled brown,

and saw her fetching them
    a cup of water

as she would not do for us,
    waking up parched,

dirtying her knees to tamp
    the soil down around them,

we feared for the sirens.
    Did we play

with our toy guns, toy
    handcuffs, that day?

So much was strange:
    Dad's voice pleading

Give me a chance
    into the phone, and then

our piggy banks broken into.
    Bulldozers were going to

raze the woods where we'd
    dragged a mattress

for a fort, fought
    slingshot crabapple wars;

she must have thought
    she'd saved some.

Didn't she know what
    I know now:

that lady's slippers will not
    thrive if transplanted,

though they might take
    years to die?

That day, though, they were
    limp by sundown,

and the three of us,
    pink from the sun,

went in and washed up
    for supper

without being called.

LEMON MERINGUE PIE

My mother was baking a lemon meringue pie
When the phone call came that her mother had died.

Glossy yellow filling cooling in its tin
On that laminate counter with the boomerang print.

I was her kitchen helper, eleven years old.
I was beating raw egg whites in a wobbly metal bowl.

Who in their right mind would link death to a pie?
Served with it for dessert, I still push it aside.

IN SUMMER MY FATHER

In summer my father came to life
like the seeds of purple clover under the lawn
like the seeds of Queen Anne's lace under roadside meadows

In summer my father stood knee-deep
in the sea that could not drown him, being born in a sailor's caul
in the bracing Atlantic, and cupped his hands and drank

In summer my father's copper freckles
merged into a tan, though my own would never do it
merged, and the golden fuzz stood up on the backs of his fingers

In summer my father grew tomatoes
setting aside his papers to stake and cage the seedlings
setting aside his cocktail and Viceroy cigarettes

And summer was the season for baseball
listening to the Red Sox on a crackling transistor radio
hearing the echoes of cheers for his hits at Melrose High School

In summer my mother took to her room with a book
complaining that she felt faint, that it might be a touch of heatstroke
complaining of poison ivy, of an ear infected from swimming

But in summer my father came to life

THE DOLLHOUSE

She was no longer a child when they gave her the dollhouse she had always coveted in childhood: three stories high, with the front wall shorn off so that she could see into every room at once. Right away she began furnishing it with tiny books of fairy tales and nursery rhymes. In one room she put some northern woods with slender birch and crabapple trees, a field of Queen Anne's lace, and a pond with ice crackling around its edges. She chose her grandmother's pale green bird-patterned wallpaper for the dining room and her aunt's wringer washing machine for the kitchen. She set a frowning mother doll in the living room and lay a handsome father doll down on the Harvest Gold sofa. In the den she placed a tin ceiling, a rainbow-colored jukebox, and a honky-tonk piano. Behind the bar she propped a boy doll with the sun's corona for a head. "Hurry up," said a voice. Quickly, she planted a sweet olive bush outside the kitchen door. She buried the bones of her favorite cat by the patio and was just about to sprinkle some morning glory seeds when the voice said, "Time's up." "Wait a sec," she said. "I still need to add these morning glories, and Vilnius in winter, and two blue parakeets, and of course, love . . ." Then suddenly she understood, without having to be told, that it was time for her to move in.

FUSION AT SEA

Those having torches will pass them on to others.
—*Plato*

Thanksgiving night on
the beach at San Clemente,
a red sun sinking,

the engineer I
was then dating said fusion's
not an option for

electric plants: you
need a source like a small sun
to get the process

going on its own.
He'd grown up playing guitar
on his dad's cruise boat

in Florida. His
mother cooked what they caught; his
sister cleaned cabins.

It's been suggested,
he said, his voice almost lost
in the surf's pounding,

that one reactor
float on a barge at sea, so
it could pull up to

plants built on coastlines,
light them off with the power of
a red star. I saw

then a vast fireball
glittering on a platform
on the wine-dark sea,

and I thought of my
teachers, most of them dead now,
each of them a sun.

LAST WORDS

W. N. T. (1944–2022)

Did the cow calf?
Those were the last coherent words
before he passed, bachelor farmer, 78.
And death for him meant no more
raising and lowering the gates
on either side of the high-speed train tracks
slicing the lane to the farm
to keep a rogue steer from getting out
times he drove the old Mercedes into town.

Did the cow calf?
Born on the family farm
but drawn to electronics in his early years,
he'd seemed an unlikely farmer.
Quaint even then, the notion of a "sense of duty,"
so when his elderly father died
many who had known him were surprised
he stepped up to take it over.

Did the cow calf?
Satisfied at the answer, he let go.
I livestreamed his funeral service
from County Mayo.
Some like the high life, said the priest,
but he was a private sort;
we must not overstep.
His brother's eulogy was short.

ELEGY FOR A PERFORMANCE ARTIST

D. C. F. (1943–2010)

Friends of yours recall
how you once got pink-slipped for
making college art

students paint with their
own shit; how you rolled onto
stage in a wheelchair,

jammed a gun to one
temple, fired it, slumped, maimed, not
knowing blanks could kill.

When your doctor-dad
sent you letters calling you
a "n'er-do-well," you

shot some full of holes,
set fire to others, then found
a trendy downtown

gallery to mount
a show, shouting "ATTENTION!"
on your megaphone.

That megaphone was
why I noticed you at a
Maple Leaf reading;

I was drunk and loved
crazy men then (still do). But
our first date began

in near-normalcy:
a Yankees exhibition
baseball game in the

Superdome, where, when
a foul ball flew into the
stands, you dove for it:

Kerplunk! heroic!
We carried that ratty ball
all night, through the bars.

Somehow that date stretched
out for days. You spun your
Rolodex in search

of Emmylou's un-
listed number—who had a
Rolodex at home,

but you? You claimed Jim
Morrison had been your friend,
then said you were Jim.

I began coming
down with something: the flu or
surreality.

When I tried to sleep,
you pried my eyelids open,
made a puppet speak.

I escaped at last,
later found in my car a
leather jacket with

a driver's license
five years older than you said.
You got let go from

UNO, went home
to Baltimore, I guess—and
then this news you'd passed.

"Rest in peace," say your
closer friends, but what I wish
for you is that you

pace in manic
agitation at the end of
a curly phone cord,

the likes of which will
also not be seen again.
You were too wild for

me in that decade
when the bucking bronco rides
in bars would fling us

mindlessly aside.
Now that I have time to sleep,
I dream you back alive.

RUBY RED OPEL GT

Your car is new.
It has A/C.
The engine's under
warranty

and yet your heart's
unmoved as stone.
You dream of one
you used to own

which (like a pet)
acquired a name—
Ruby, her color
red as flame,

the hue your Mom
warned not to wear
because it clashed
with your flaming hair.

Her headlight-eyes
were lidded shut,
recessed in the hood
till a lever was tugged

in hard reverse.
So cool! So what,
in the moonless dark,
if they sometimes stuck?

And what if she wasn't
built to stop?
Idling too long
caused vapor-lock,

the engine flooded.
She loved to *go,*
and when she wouldn't,
some knight would show

and give her a push.
(You were pretty then,
your body unmarred
by nicks and dents.)

Now that Sir Galahads
are few,
a Triple-A card
rescues you

when in distress—
a punctured tread
the worst malfunction
one might dread.

But in the past
a cloud of steam
pours from a hood
as in a dream

(your flame-red roadster
running hot),
and you relearn
what you forgot,

driving in comfort
with a spare:
Risk was the road
to everywhere.

JEEP PANTOUM

The first time we drove home from Shreveport in your Jeep
we were talking so intensely, we overshot our exit
Not by one exit, but by twenty-something miles
My eyes had been locked on your Roman-coin profile

You were talking so intensely, you overshot our exit
after listening to a Beatles tribute band in Shreveport
Riding home, eyes locked on your Roman-coin profile
was like being twelve years old with my first crush, on Paul

We'd been listening to a copycat concert in Shreveport
but they didn't play my favorite, "We Can Work It Out"
What age is the cutoff for an adolescent crush?
Not sixty, so it must be some number beyond that

They didn't play my favorite, "We Can Work It Out"
which I'm hearing in my mind as I go about my business
Your Jeep climbed from 60 to 75
as we rode home in silence, the exit a relief

What I'm thinking today as I go about my business:
How strange to retrace the same stretch of a highway
but speed along in silence, the exit a relief
the last time we rode home from Shreveport in your Jeep

ATTENUATION

How is it that the two of us took up
less mattress space than either one apart,
despite three kitty-cats (but not the dog)
nestling in the gaps of body parts?
And then the loveseat where we watched TV
would not support a midget lying prone,
but seemed to bear our bodies comfortably
when curving flesh to flesh and bone to bone.
I think there's some dimension where we slipped
when touching all the way from heads to toes,
though you (a skeptic and a scientist)
would scoff at that. I know no matter goes
from this expanding universe we're in,
but, dear: together we grew awfully thin.

COLORIFIC

Gold stud earrings
shaped like hearts,
an ice-blue satin nightgown:
he always gave
the most romantic presents,
the way he'd tuck
a love note in with her
brown-bag lunch.

So when that nest of
crumpled tissue paper
parted to reveal
a red-brown raincoat—
sensible and high-necked,
one size too big—
she saw at once
what it meant.

That boxed raincoat
was the color of
dead leaves in the gutter;
picked scabs;
cranberry bogs in winter;
and soggy puddings
baked of flour,
eggs, and blood.

THE PALE GREEN MOTH

The pale green moth landed in the crook of her left elbow, on a spot where she liked to dab perfume. She worried that a sudden movement would startle it, but it stayed put, even when she went to sleep that night and woke up the next morning. In the shower, she was careful to hold her left arm out of the water stream. She started to put on a sleeveless summer blouse, but it was cold outside and drafty in the old house, so instead she cut the sleeve off her least-favorite sweater. The moth ate a crumb of English muffin for breakfast. Right from the beginning, she could feel her love for the moth and the moth's love for her flowing back and forth between them, like thick amber honey coating the sides of a glass pipe. *Don't think you have to just sit there, for my sake,* she thought. *You could fly.* No sooner had the thought formed in her mind than the pale green moth rose straight up in the air, hovered above her elbow for a second or two, and then re-alighted on its home spot.

That's how she discovered that the moth would follow her thought-commands. It would fly to the window and back, or in a spiral nebula pattern—whatever she could imagine it doing. She cut the left sleeves off her entire wardrobe and fashioned a tiny water bowl from a bottle-cap. She and the moth were like two countries with an ocean between them, wave after wave of fierce, unrelenting love crashing on their opposing shores. Then one day she woke up cross. *I'm tired of wearing lopsided clothes,* she thought. *I want to wear bell sleeves, bishop's sleeves, kimono sleeves, French cuffs.* She glanced at the pale green moth, which was resting there unsuspecting, humming with love for her. *I could kill it,* she thought. "Oh, God!" she cried. But it was too late.

THE LEMON JUICE ALPHABET

In the recurring dream, you are reading over the page you have just written, certain that it is what you have been trying to say all your life, that you finally got it right. As you read, though, the words begin fading. That's when you realize you are dreaming, that it is necessary to memorize the lines in order to carry them back with you to the waking world. You squint, to better focus on the words as they are graying out. But the page has gone blank. Back in sixth grade, at your best friend's house, the two of you used to pen secret messages with a watercolor brush dipped in lemon juice. The writing would be invisible until the sheet of paper was held over the flame of a gas stove. Then ghostly letters of the alphabet would begin appearing, just as a lick of flame would shoot up to ignite the page, whoosh, and you would have to let it go—let go and watch it burn to blackened scraps on the stovetop next to a plastic-wrapped plate of your friend's grandmother's kolaches, those hardened lumps of dough brought back from another vanished world.

AKHMATOVA

St. Petersburg, Russia

Though Pushkin monuments were everywhere,
It took some time to find the right address
Where Stalin caged her like a lioness.
The courtyard trees (her only view) were bare.
Indoors: a shabby couch, a desk, a chair,
And two more images of Pushkin's face
Invading even her domestic space—
I guess it gave her hope to see him there.
Imagine thirty years of house arrest
Made somehow bearable by books and art,
The silver icon of the chilled dawn kiss.
Before my own home country fell apart—
It makes me so ashamed, admitting this—
I envied her that subject matter's heft.

BASS VOICE

Walking by the Polish church in Vilnius one Sunday morning, she is arrested by the sound of a male voice, singing over the choir. So deep, so resonant, so mournful: surely it must belong to an opera star. She stands transfixed outside, then pushes a heavy wooden door to get in. But now the voice seizes her, shakes her like a mouse in the jaws of a cat. She hurries across the lobby space and pauses by an icon shop tucked in one corner, where she can peer through an archway into the gilt dazzle of the church proper. The pews are full, and behind them is a sea of kerchief-headed women, kneeling on the stone floor. But who owns the voice, and where is it coming from? She would have to walk partway down the aisle in her blue jeans, then turn brazenly around and look up, up, into the organ loft. Rude, yes: but she has no choice against the power of that voice. But now the clerk who has been minding the rosaries and scapulars begins squawking and flapping like a sparrow, cursing a young woman who rushes out of the shop. The clerk points to her purse, a shoulder bag, and when she looks down she sees that it is unzipped all the way, with one corner of her wallet poking out. She grabs the wallet and counts her litas—all there, thankfully. "Ačiū," she tells the clerk, then thinks maybe she should buy something, but is that proper during church? But by then the voice has stopped singing, releasing her from its spell, and she is free to stagger on wobbly legs out into the weak rays of the Baltic sun. And perhaps it is better that way, to exist on the cusp of probability, owning every story ending at once.

PECAN TREE STORIES

1.

"Don't place your picnic table
under a pecan tree," goes the old
Cajun saying. Must be an Anglo
who planted this one next to my house
a hundred years ago. Pecan wood's
brittle, and when a hard rain soaks
limbs heavy with green pecans,
you never know when one will *crack,*
crash down on something—
last year my paid-for car,
totaled right in my driveway,
garlanded with boughs of greenery
like a float on Mardi Gras Day.

2.

At daybreak after Hurricane Rita,
my yard looked like Birnam Wood
advancing: limbs and branches down
everywhere, a solid mass of green.
That's when the neighbors told me
that the lot across the street
used to have a house like mine,
crushed by a pecan tree.

3.

Living with a pecan tree means
living with the *ping, ping*
of ripe pecans on corrugated tin,
the garage roof
under continual shelling

when they're in season;
and the doorbell ringing,
hauling you out of a late-day nap
to some tattered old man with a grocery sack
wanting to pick your pecans.

4.

Next time the house sells,
the buyer might have to chop the tree down
to get insurance on it—
that's what happened up the street.
But a tree grows as dear as family.
If forced to, could I destroy it?
There are women who must chop their breasts off
because they might get cancer,
and a woman who makes pro-and-con lists
about a deceitful lover
with a sweet tooth for pecan pralines.

5.

Everything's coming into leaf this week
except the old pecan trees:
the Japanese magnolias raining down pink,
a light purple fuzz on the redbuds.
But the old pecans won't leaf
until the freeze danger's finally over,
and the local farmers trust them
for not being tricked into hope.

AFTERMATH

Against strong odds, a
rain-soaked pecan limb came down
during the freak storm

just as Pumpkin, my
ten-month-old kitten,
was heading for the

shelter of the porch.
Only cat I'd let go out
these past thirty years;

too full of life for
my Victorian cottage;
not killed but blinded

by the Jove-hurled bolt.
Brain concussion, said the vet.
Some peripheral

vision returning;
shouldn't get your hopes up yet.
Eyes dull as amber.

Home now, he's a heat-
seeking missile locked on my
coordinates as

I move room to room;
doesn't even try to slip
out the screen door to

the lush world I couldn't
keep him from before; time
cleaved into *then* and

now by that dropped limb
the way the green wood will cleave
with each hatchet blow

when my yardman comes
to chop and haul. Too close to
home, these days, skies fall.

THE TREE KEEPS WEEPING

The tree keeps weeping where a limb broke off.
When I say "limb"—it was a Frankenstein.
The crash woke me and the entire block.
The limb took down a live electric line.
How long before its histrionics stop?
For three weeks now the tree has carried on,
The limb long sawn in chunks and carted off,
And still its black tears puddle on my lawn.
"Stop sniveling!" I'd like to tell the tree:
"The victims here are all the insects caught
Like those in amber from the Baltic Sea"—
As if an old pecan cared what I thought,
As if I hadn't wept a sea of salt
For situations that were all my fault.

PINK MAGNOLIA

Every spring I try
to photograph my pink
magnolia tree in bloom,

but the angles aren't
right—either the sun's blazing
or the pink looks drab.

Focus on the lace
abstract patterns and miss those
goblet-shaped blossoms;

zoom for a close-up
and miss that pink filigree
on powder-blue sky.

Carpet of petals
the shade of my peppermint
lipstick in 8th grade,

sweetness in the air
thick as grandmother's perfume
or Lenten incense . . .

Foolish to want to
get it into one still frame.
A lifetime, trying.

MIMOSA

I know what tree I
want to plant by the dogwood
stump: a mimosa—

not the Old World shrub
the champagne cocktail's named for,
cultivated for

its yellow blossoms
in the south of France, but the
common trash tree that

plants itself like a
lunar flagpole along the
meanest highways in

Louisiana.
When it blooms: pink silk starbursts,
the whole yard perfumed,

before it begins
dropping pink rot and seedpods
to remind us that

what we'll remember
best at the end of life is
what's sticky and smells.

CANE

St. Gabriel, Louisiana

This time of year
the cane trucks—

open-slatted like
circus wagons,

dribbling stalks
along the shoulder—

wobble along the rural
highway by the river,

backing up cars.
The air's charred

with the rumlike
sweetness of scorched cane.

Clouds of egrets
drift behind a thresher.

The children down here
suck sugarcane stalks,

but where I grew up's
too cold for this crop,

too cold for my heart.

ACROSS A CROWDED ROOM

It's the fault of those Broadway musicals on my mother's hi-fi
that I half-expected my fellow drunks to burst into song
(cue "Some Enchanted Evening" from *South Pacific*)
the night you walked into the room at my AA home group

I half-expected my fellow drunks to burst into song
while an orchestra rose from the church basement floor
the night you walked into the room at my AA home group
Love at first sight may just be remembering the future

A tall, skinny black-haired man walks into a church basement
and time stops, a heart stops, a mouth drops open
Love at first sight may just be remembering the birth room
Someone imprinted on us before we were conscious

Time stops, a heart stops, a mouth drops open
once in every musical, that showstopping moment
when rationality yields to the pull of the unconscious
I was raised on Broadway musicals from my mother's hi-fi

EVERY MARDI GRAS DAY

Every Mardi Gras Day we would go to that stiff party
Thrown by a member of the Landrieu family:
Not sweet Mayor Moon, who had integrated the city,
But the one with a gun shop in Kenner or Metairie.

We'd stand on our feet for hours on the roped-off lawn
(A hired security guard ejecting would-be crashers)
As Rex lumbered by with its dewy debutante queen
And paunchy businessman king as old as her father.

I'd get my revenge at the poetry readings
You'd sit through confused but gallantly polite.
Your uptown friends were appalled by my lack of proper breeding.
My poet friends were convinced you were not too bright.

Not even I believed that we would last this long,
But "If Ever I Cease to Love" was Rex's song.

WATER IN THE AIR

You were obsessed with putting water in the air:
the air too dry inside my house, you said.
You'd rise and put a pot of water on the stove
while I still slept.

Twice, when I woke and went to make coffee,
the pot was scorched black, all the water boiled out,
and you fast asleep on my living room sofa
snoring, open mouthed.

But you could turn any fight or sore subject
into a joke, even a scare like that,
making a funny face and hissing "Water in the air!"
to make me laugh.

Where you live now, you're locked out of the kitchen.
They bring you your meals on a tray at fixed times.
The air reeks of Lysol and overnight diapers.
How did I miss the signs?

NULER

I was happy all day today because you called me "Nuler,"
pulling that pet name out of the depths of memory.
Sometimes, in our brief phone calls, I can't help but wonder
if you know who I am or if it's like ChatGPT.

My late mom was the only one who called me "Wooie."
A late boss was the only one who called me "Fox."
They took those pet names with them to the cemetery,
but you'll probably still be alive when "Nuler" is lost.

In that fairy tale with the maid spinning straw into gold,
Rumpelstiltskin disappears when she utters his secret name;
but I think they got it backward, so very long ago.
What did the Brothers Grimm really know about pain?

Some part of us does disappear when a magic spell is broken,
but it happens when a secret name *stops* being spoken

THE OLD IRISH HARPERS

Those were not the instruments
of angels up in clouds
but of human beings
blinded by smallpox
Their hearing grown sharp as a fox's
Their nails grown long as the talons of eagles
to pluck strings of brass or silver
that would cut modern fingertips like razors

The last of them
Denis Hempson from Magilligan
Taught by Bridget O'Cahan
He lived to one hundred and eleven
Now he's buried in St. Aidan's
with the bones of my O'Cahans

And his songs are just symbols on a page
Oh I could steal a sallow harp
from a glass museum case
I could sharpen my fingernails
to quill-points

But who is left to teach me to play
those strings that ring like bells
but cut like knives,
the music of the old Irish harpers?